WITH LOVE FROM HEAVEN

LILLY P.

TATE PUBLISHING
AND **ENTERPRISES**, LLC

Scripture quotations marked (ESV) are from *The Holy Bible, English Standard Version®*, copyright © 2001 by Crossway Bibles, a publishing ministry of Good News Publishers. Used by permission. All rights reserved.

Scripture quotations marked (KJV) are taken from the *Holy Bible, King James Version*, Cambridge, 1769. Used by permission. All rights reserved.

Scripture quotations marked (NIV) are taken from the *Holy Bible, New International Version®*, NIV®. Copyright © 1973, 1978, 1984 by Biblica, Inc.™ Used by permission of Zondervan. All rights reserved worldwide. www.zondervan.com

Scripture quotations marked (NKJV) are taken from the *New King James Version*. Copyright © 1982 by Thomas Nelson, Inc. Used by permission. All rights reserved.

This novel is a work of fiction. Names, descriptions, entities, and incidents included in the story are products of the author's imagination. Any resemblance to actual persons, events, and entities is entirely coincidental.

The opinions expressed by the author are not necessarily those of Tate Publishing, LLC.

Published by Tate Publishing & Enterprises, LLC
127 E. Trade Center Terrace | Mustang, Oklahoma 73064 USA
1.888.361.9473 | www.tatepublishing.com

Tate Publishing is committed to excellence in the publishing industry. The company reflects the philosophy established by the founders, based on Psalm 68:11,
"The Lord gave the word and great was the company of those who published it."

Book design copyright © 2016 by Tate Publishing, LLC. All rights reserved.
Cover design by Albert Ceasar Compay
Interior design by Mary Jean Archival

Published in the United States of America

ISBN: 978-1-68293-013-7
1. Fiction / Christian / General
2. Fiction / Religious
16.04.06

Acknowledgments

To Jesus Christ
My Dad for repairing my computer,
which allowed me to finish this manuscript

Preface

On August 6, 2012, I lost my former associate pastor to cancer. After spending the night in prayer, not only was my writing ability restored (it was taken away for lack of use), but I also began writing a story about heaven.

What can those who've never been to heaven know about it, you may ask? Well, doesn't the Bible say, "Eye hath not seen, nor ear heard, neither have entered into the heart of man, the things which God hath prepared for them that love Him" (1 Cor. 2:9, KJV)? I caution my readers not to take scripture out of context. This verse can only be understood correctly in the light of the following verse, 1 Corinthians 2:10 (KJV), which reads, "But God revealed them unto us by his Spirit: for the Spirit searcheth all things, yea, the deep things of God."

My purpose in writing about heaven is to comfort those who read this story, especially those grieving from the loss of a loved one. The brief mention of hell here is necessary lest we believe something that is not biblical about it. (It's not there.

I'm a good person, so I won't go there.) Scaring people for the sake of a fear-based thrill is demonic.

> For the Spirit God gave us does not make us timid, but gives us power, love and self-discipline. (2 Tim. 1:7, NIV)

Readers, I believe that Christ and my love for you demand that I mention hell briefly so that you won't end up down there with no way to ever get out. Talking about it briefly in this book might just save you an eternity of endless terror and torment.

Christ has given each person freedom to choose a life with Him or without Him. He will respect whatever choice is made by each individual. He will never override the devastating consequences of someone's rejection of Him.

You were created for a personal relationship with Jesus Christ so you can enjoy His love forever. What choice will you make regarding Jesus Christ? Please consider seriously and carefully. Your eternity is at stake.

Pastor Ansel at Home

Pastor Ansel Almstedt stood on a long winding staircase and looked at an oil painting of him and his family on the wall above the railing. Next to that was the photograph that the artist had used as a reference. He realized that on earth, the photograph would be a negative image.

He heard the Holy Spirit say, "Write down everything you see and do as though you were talking to Lydia." Pastor Ansel picked up a small cloth-covered blank book that was on the fourth landing. Pastor Ansel described the painting as a wonderful likeness of his family. It was one of their last Christmas' together.

Pastor Ansel smiled as he thought of Lydia, her bangs combed back with just a touch of starch, framing her forehead on each side like little wings. Her fiery-red tresses hung down in long, thick waves. When her temper flared, her pretty cream-colored, egg-shaped countenance matched her hair. She had a quick temper, but very rarely did it flare; and on those infrequent occasions, her thunder passes quickly. He missed holding her face in his hands and running his fingers through her hair. Though those in heaven missed their loved ones on earth, they weren't sad.

Lydia's sea-blue eyes sparkled, especially when she laughed. She was joyful, even after his cancer diagnosis. As Baptists, he and Lydia believed in supernatural healing on earth. Gradually though, they both realized that his (Pastor Ansel's) healing was not to be. His "victorian doll," as he called Lydia, had a long, narrow, pointed nose that twitched right before she sobbed. Lydia, like Pastor Ansel, had short, thin lips and smiles that lit any room they walked into. Lydia was 5'3" tall. She had a petite build and weighed approximately 115 pounds soaking wet.

Suddenly there was a bright, blinding pillar of light beside him, and it radiated tremendous heat. He realized that inside the light was Jesus Christ. Pastor Ansel fell to his knees and kissed the exposed part of the Lord's feet. Looking up, still kneeling, he saw that the pillar of light had disappeared; then he saw that the Lord's whole body was visible.

Jesus was six feet tall. He had medium-brown, shoulder-length hair feathered above His short forehead, which appeared as though it rose to a point where the center of

His bangs would be (that is, if He had them). His eyebrows were black, thick on the outside and narrowing sharply at the top of His long, slender nose, which spreads out slightly at the bottom. His jawline (Pastor Ansel would discover later) was shorter and more chiseled than his mother's. He had a mustache and closely cropped beard that covered His cheeks and His small, square chin.

Pastor Ansel was captivated, first, by the Lord's eyes (they were green). Still in silent rapture, Pastor Ansel saw the wounds in His wrists and feet. Jesus wore a long, white robe with a golden sash stretching from His left shoulder then looped around on His right hip. Jesus showed Pastor Ansel that their first face-to-face encounter had been described in its entirety by Christ from His precious son's perspective.

"I knew you'd be overwhelmed." The Lord laughed tenderly. The Lord placed His right hand on Pastor Ansel's left shoulder. "Well done, good and faithful servant. Welcome home."

Jesus. It's really You, thought Pastor Ansel, still awed by the sight of the Lord.

"Yes, it's Me. Here, kiss the whole foot," said Christ, laughing, guiding Pastor Ansel off the stairs. He kicked off one sandal and then the other.

Pastor Ansel smiled, picked up Jesus's right foot, stroked it gently, and kissed the wound; then he repeated the same process with the other foot.

"Do you like them?" asked Jesus, gesturing toward the wall, seeing Pastor Ansel still in silent rapture.

Yes, they're beautiful! thought Pastor Ansel.

There was a mirror to the right of the portrait. He backed up to get a better look at himself. He stood 5'9" tall and had a round cut to his auburn hair and a handlebar mustache of the same color. Though he was fifty-one, he had the look of someone half his age. His bald spot and receding hairline were not there. The beautiful white robe he wore on his slender frame fit well and felt comfortable.

"What's the sash for?" asked Pastor Ansel.

"That signifies rank," explained the Lord. "Each color is a different level. Red is high."

In Revelation, it says that your hair is white, thought Pastor Almstedt.

"You think I should look old while everyone else in heaven is young?" Jesus teased.

"No, Lord, I just…It's just that Scripture says…"

"Easy, Son. I know you want to be true to what the Bible says. When the Apostle John saw Me in the fullness of My glory, what was his first response?"

"Fear," said Pastor Ansel. A light suddenly went on in his head.

"There will be many times you will see Me here like that but not for our first face-to-face encounter."

The fullness of Your glory makes Your hair look *white?* concluded Pastor Ansel, without words.

"Yes," answered Christ.

"Jesus, can I give you a hug?"

"Why, Ansel Almstedt, I do believe you've found your voice! Yes, give me a hug. I'd like that very much. I was waiting for you to ask Me. You've wanted to ever since you saw Me."

The two men embraced.

"Let's talk some more about the painting."

"It's signed Lloyd Peace. Is he any relation to Lilly? I want to thank him."

"Lloyd is her grandpa."

"How did he get a picture of me and my family?"

"I can do miracles, so getting a picture of you and your family for Lloyd was not a problem. 'For nothing will be impossible with God'" quoted Jesus in Luke 1:37 (ESV).

"Lord, may I ask You something?"

"Sure, anything."

"I don't ask for myself. I'm in the third heaven. It's for the sake of my family."

Jesus's expression became very serious because He knew what was coming.

"Why did I get cancer? I'm sorry if it's not my place to ask."

"Oh no, Ansel. It's all right to ask. Remember, I asked My Father three separate times in the garden to make it possible for Me to skip going to the cross, even though I knew it was My Father's will that I die to remove the curse of original sin."

"'My Father, if it be possible, let this cup pass from Me: nevertheless not as I will, but as thou wilt'" quoted Pastor Ansel; then he went on. "'God made Him who had no sin to

be sin for us, so that in him we might become the righteous-
ness of God'"

"Right, Ansel," said Christ. "You know your Bible."

"I should know the Scriptures. I'm a pastor," the Lord's
companion concluded laughingly.

"This journal is a gift to Lydia describing your life here in
heaven until the time of her arrival. Everyone with loved ones
in heaven will receive one of these journals."

"You can tell Lydia in that journal that if you're agreeable
to it, after you're settled here, I would like you to teach some
pastors for Me. Contrary to the assumption of most people,
the fact that someone graduated from seminary doesn't
necessarily make them a Christian or a good pastor."

Jesus knew that Pastor Ansel was thinking about His
crucifixion.

"The physical pain of being crucified was intense. From
the sharp stabbing pain in my wrists and arms to an equally
terrible similar pain in My legs and feet—not to mention
gradually suffocating…Dying is not easy. The human mind
goes into survival mode, so there's always a struggle to release
the spirit, even for Me. But the worst part for Me was being
denied by the Father.

I was going to wait till after Rose and Lloyd went home to
have your review, if that's all right with you?"

"Whatever you like." Pastor Ansel shrugged, smiling.

"Most of your works survived."

"What do you mean by most?"

"I mean, Ansel, my friend, that everyone—except Me—has at least some works that are burned because they're only human."

"Will any sin affect me in the works judgment?"

"You finished well. Don't be concerned...You asked me before about why you had cancer. One reason is so you could empathize with other people who have it on earth or came here because of it. The second reason that I can tell you about is upstairs in your den. I was going to show you the lower floors first, but because you mentioned your cancer, that takes priority."

The Lord regarded Pastor Ansel with tenderness as He watched him run effortlessly up the next floor to his den. Christ opened the door and they walked in together. Inside a case in a large drawer was a beautiful three-tiered crown made of a precious metal only found in heaven.

Picking up the journal, Pastor Ansel wrote, "Lydia, it's awesome. The crown of life has rubies and white and black pearls. It looks delicate but not feminine...There are many other crowns, Lydia. I was surprised to find out how many crowns I've got."

"Getting back to what I was saying about training the pastors, you'd be surprised how many don't know what the Bible says till they come here," explained Christ.

"I was blessed to have a colleague who knows the Bible well."

"Yeah, I'm not worried about Brent Walker."

"I was concerned about him while I had cancer. He carried so much more of the workload at Jesus, Friend of Sinners Baptist Church," said Pastor Ansel. "Lord, please bless, heal, and keep Pastor Brent Walker and his wife, Sophia. He needs wisdom, strength, and rest. She needs the same in addition to physical healing for her heart. I'd like you to bless, heal, and keep my family. Be a husband to Lydia, a father to my sons, John and Alex, and a father to my daughter-in-law Grace."

Pastor Ansel remembered his eldest son, John, and his wife at their wedding. His handsome firstborn had dark-brown hair and eyes. John looked nothing like him or Lydia. He was a captain in the army, so against his will, he had a crew cut. He had a low forehead like the Lord, no beard but the same short jawline. His sparsely freckled face had a curved chin. He was friendly and extraverted.

Grace Almstedt had a pageboy cut to her strawberry-blond hair. Pastor Ansel often joked that she looked more like his younger son, Alex, and his wife, Lydia, than she did her immediate family. Her face was oval, and an abundance of orange freckles dotted it. She had hazel eyes. Alex was only a head taller than his sister-in-law. She was congenial, like John, though more reserved.

"Yes, that's a wonderful prayer. Thank you, Ansel. I'll consider everything you've said in accordance with My will."

"I've decided to teach those pastors. Please tell me about them so I know what to expect from each one."

"Stephen Kent won't believe there's a hell when he goes back to earth. I tried to reach him on that issue every nice way I could, but he insists on telling his congregation that there is no hell.

"Patrick Sheldon believes in hell but says it's only for people like Hitler. If these two and Sam Gibbons don't come around to My way of thinking with your help, I'm gonna scare them straight. They have to believe more than the existence of hell.

"They have to believe their congregation members and visitors are going there if they don't receive Me as their personal Savior. Samuel Wilson had all his works burned. He did good works, but they weren't done to my glory," explained Christ. "Here's a list of names of the whole class, including the ones I've told you about. We'll talk more about it later.

Let me show you more of this mansion before we talk further about business."

"I want to thank Lloyd."

"That can be arranged. Lloyd and Rose will be along in about an hour. Remember, this is your home."

Suddenly an angel appeared, smiling pleasantly at Jesus and Pastor Ansel.

"Tell us at any time during this tour if there's anything you don't like, and we'll change it," continued Christ.

"I'm not sure how I know this, Lydia, but I've just met my guardian angel," Pastor Ansel wrote in the journal. "His name is Herman."

"There's immediate recognition here," said the Lord.

Pastor Ansel looked up with a smile. He added, "Jesus is putting me to work, Lydia. I'm gonna be teaching prodigals. I know in my heart that work in heaven is not the toil and tedium it is on earth."

"You have a desk here by the east window so you can see the sunrise from the heavens. I know you expressed concern to Lydia that you would never see a sunrise. There's a leather swivel chair with wheels, a hibiscus on the desk, a fern in the west corner. Right by the fern is a reclining couch."

"Everything is fine, except I think I'd like the plants hung on hooks from the ceiling to free up desk and floor space."

"There's a couple more things in here that will interest you. There's a computer in here on the desk, a laptop in the pencil drawer, a cell phone, and a signet ring.

"One thing everyone needs to understand about the third heaven is that morally the glorified church is old-fashioned *on purpose*. But as far as technology is concerned, we're way ahead of earth."

There was a computer on the desk with a recessed book shelf behind it. It held many Bibles, reference books, fiction and nonfiction titles.

"You have a library right next door too," said the Lord.

In addition to similar titles like those in the den, Pastor Ansel found many of the famous classics, some of which were children's books. There was also a media center.

"What are the children's books for?" asked Pastor Ansel.

"Quite often the kids will stop by and want someone to read to them. There are other options to reading a hard copy. Turn on an audiobook, or let them use the history/future observatory. The whole Bible, for example, can be viewed as though it's currently happening. Past, present, and future on earth and in heaven can be seen as though it were occurring now. You'll also see how people here respond to those on earth."

"I'd like to see how that works," Pastor Ansel mused. "My son Alex would enjoy seeing this part of my library."

Pastor Ansel pondered the younger of his two sons for a minute. Alex was tall and gangly, surpassing both him and Lydia in height. He was awkward and shy around strangers, but once he got to know you, he was warm and fun. He was nineteen at the time of Pastor Ansel's death. Unlike his parents, he had a long, wide smile. His strawberry-blond hair was styled in a bob and had a cowlick. He was an artist.

"Watch while I program this system so you can work it out yourself."

Jesus unlocked a panel in the wall and pressed a few buttons. Suddenly Queen Esther appeared before them, in front of their eyes, and invited Hamen and the King to a banquet.

"This device is also used for your review. Everyone has one, but only your review is programmed into your system.

"When the children use this alone, I want you to block things like Judas's suicide. They have been taught the Scripture, so they know how he died. They don't need to see it."

"What about the drowning of the Egyptians?" asked Pastor Ansel.

"I'll let that go," replied Christ. "Why don't we go into one of the living rooms?"

Pastor Ansel was silent for a while, taking in his immediate surroundings. Inside the enormous room was (clockwise) a beige couch, a tan sectional, a brown leather chair, an overstuffed light-blue chair. Next to that were an aisle and a white Queen Anne wing chair while on the other side of the foyer was another desk—a roll top. It was open, revealing another desktop computer.

"We have internet here in heaven. Here's a complete list of everyone's e-mail address."

There was an open space, and completing the circle, nearest the door was a light-blue Hide-a-Bed.

2

Neighbors

Just then the doorbell rang.

"That would be Rose and Lloyd," said Jesus. "Should I let them in?"

"Yes, that would be fine," replied Pastor Ansel. He jotted a few more things about the room in the journal he was keeping for Lydia.

"We were just about to discuss the crucifixion," Jesus explained to Pastor Ansel's guests as He led them up to the living room on the fifth floor. "Pastor Ansel Almstedt, these are Lilly's grandparents, Lloyd—"

Lilly's grandma ran forward and hugged Pastor Ansel, interrupting Jesus as he was making introductions. "It's so nice to meet Lilly's pastor!"

"And Rose Peace." Jesus laughed tenderly.

Christ gave both Lloyd and Rose a hug then kissed Rose on the check. Each of them had a short haircut and a hairstyle of about the late 1920s, Pastor Ansel guessed.

Rose stood about 5'5" tall. Lloyd was half a head taller than Rose. Lloyd had a forehead slightly higher than his former wife's. His face was oblong at the top and gradually changed to oval below his hazel eyes. His lips, though slightly thicker than Rose's, were not disproportional. Rose had delicate facial features—a normal eye frame with soft hazel eyes, a short-though-not-a-pug nose, and lips that were neither too narrow nor too thick but were in exact proportion to her very feminine oval face.

"Thank you for your kind words and for the hug Rose, but I'm afraid I can't be much of a shepherd to your granddaughter from here. I can and do pray for her," responded Pastor Almstedt.

Rose's sash is olive green while Lloyd's is blue, Pastor Ansel noted silently.

"Lloyd, you're an excellent artist. Thank you for decorating the fourth floor staircase wall and this room of my home with your fine work."

"Here are a couple more paintings you'll enjoy," interjected Christ. "One is a self-portrait. Next to that, we have another Lloyd Peace original."

"You in Gethsemane," observed Pastor Almstedt.

"Right. What else do you notice about it?" asked the Lord with a barely contained smile.

"Wait," said Pastor Ansel suddenly, "that's Herman!"

"Yes, I was wondering how long it would take you to see that." Christ chuckled.

"You gave me the angel who comforted You the night You were betrayed. Thank you, Lord. That's very thoughtful... Lord, thank You for dying for me and for being resurrected for me too. I would have mentioned it before but..."

"You were overwhelmed." Jesus laughed tenderly. "I have that effect on people."

"Jesus, will You tell us more about your crucifixion?" asked Pastor Ansel.

"It was a miserable day right from the start," Christ began. "The only redeeming aspect of the crucifixion—no pun intended—was that after it was carried out, I wouldn't have to surrender my disciples to hell."

"'Fixing our eyes on Jesus, the pioneer and perfecter of our faith. For the joy set before him he endured the cross, scorning its shame, and sat down at the right hand of the throne of God'" quoted Pastor Ansel.

"Exactly!" said the Lord.

"'Just as there were many who were appalled at Him—his appearance was so disfigured beyond that of any human being and his form marred beyond human likeness [Isa. 52:14],'" quoted Pastor Ansel again.

"Have You showed Pastor Ansel Your back yet?" asked Lloyd.

"He's told me about it." Pastor Ansel sighed.

Jesus was suddenly standing in nothing but a loincloth, turning His back toward the three of them. Rose and Pastor Ansel gasped, and Lloyd exhaled long and hard.

Lloyd suddenly blurted angrily, "Did those soldiers get away with treating your precious, sacred back like a piece of meat?"

"They did," admitted the Lord. "I had to suffer in order to make it possible to offer salvation to those who would receive Me as their Savior."

Rose regained her composure enough to say, "Lord, you told Lloyd when He first saw You that there were shards of steel woven into the leather whip."

"Right. That's what ripped my flesh down to the muscle. Eventually, I was too weak to raise Myself up so that My diaphragm could expand, allowing Myself to take a breath."

"You suffocated," concluded Pastor Ansel, realizing anew the enormity of what it cost Christ to obtain salvation.

Christ suddenly appeared in His robe again.

"Ansel," said Jesus, "Mother wants to know if she can come over. I told her you might want to get settled first."

"No, that's all right. I've wanted to see many people from the Bible."

Mary suddenly came through the wall.

"Mother, please use the door. Till he gets settled, I think it would be more polite."

"All right, Son."

"Hello, Mary. It's nice to meet you." Pastor Ansel grinned.

"Hello, Pastor Ansel. Tell them about the horse, Son," said Mary.

"Pastor Ansel doesn't like horses," the Lord chided playfully.

"I don't like to ride them, Lord, but I don't mind a story."

"It was the day before my crucifixion," Jesus began. "I told a centurion I needed to borrow his horse for the day."

"Mary is lying on a long, red cushion with a small pillow, of the same color, attached at one end. Her hair is dark brown," wrote Pastor Ansel, "tied in a ponytail down the length of her back. She is wearing a hot-pink dress. Her large, almond-colored eyes regarded Jesus with pride, the kind only a godly mother can reflect.

"Below the eyes of her oval face are high cheekbones. She has a long, narrow, pointed nose. Her jawline is long, coming to a clearly defined point at her chin. She stands 5'3" tall and has a large bright smile. Her poise is evident to everyone in the room."

Jesus continued, "He told me, 'Tomorrow, I have to kill You, but I guess it would be all right if You borrowed my horse for the day.'"

"Did he really say that, Lord?" asked Rose.

"Yes, Rose, he did. Wait, there's more. It gets better. Not only did I get to spend the day with a very compassionate animal, but that centurion also repented while I was hanging on the cross, and he later became my disciple. You remember from the Bible, Rose? 'Surely this was a righteous man'"

"He's *that* soldier?" asked Lloyd sounding amazed.

"Yes. Would you like to meet him?" asked Christ.

"All right," said the Lord's three friends though Rose and Lloyd were somewhat reluctant.

Jesus took His cell phone out of the pocket of His tunic, looked up the number of Marcus Bescelli, and called him. It wasn't long before the humble soldier was at the front door of Pastor Ansel's mansion.

"Marcus," said Jesus, "we were just about to discuss the resurrection. You know Rose and Lloyd from before, but Pastor Ansel just arrived today."

"Glad to meet you, Pastor Almstedt. I pray that the five of you will consider yourselves welcome in my home any time. Sorry to interrupt. The resurrection is one of my favorite topics, especially since I had a hand in Jesus's death. I was devastated to find out I'd killed a man who was not only innocent but God too."

"Remember what the Apostle Paul said," the Heavenly Father remarked. "'Brothers and sisters, I do not consider myself yet to have taken hold of it. But one thing I do: Forgetting what is behind and straining toward what is ahead.'"

"Yes, Abba," said Marcus. "Thank You for the reminder."

Then he turned to Rose and said, "Ma'am, I know you don't like me, but I hope someday that will change."

"Forgive me if I seem cold," said Rose. "I should remember what Paul said and not hold you to something that the Lord has forgiven. I do love you, Marcus."

Rose allowed Marcus to take both her hands in his rough and manly ones. She and Lloyd shared a loveseat.

"Getting back to the resurrection," continued Christ.

"Yes, tell us about that," said Rose, feeling a rush of joy.

"I was so elated to be united with the Father again. I'm the only one who can really describe the level of ecstasy I felt, so I brought some Bibles for each of us so that we can better understand our subject. Let's open to Matthew 28:8. Lloyd, would you please read for us?"

"Yes, Lord, I would be glad to."

He read, "'So the women hurried away from the tomb, afraid yet filled with joy, and ran to tell his disciples.'"

"Jesus, in Mark, Luke, and John, there were *two* angels. Why is there only one in Matthew? [Matthew 28:2 KJV]" asked Lloyd.

"Actually, there were *three*. Two inside the tomb, seen by John, Peter, Luke, and Mary Magdalene. Matthew didn't go in, so he only saw one," explained Christ.

"Don't write in the Bible, Lloyd," Rose scolded mildly.

"Ansel, show Rose your Bible."

Pastor Ansel did as the Lord asked. Rose stared in horror and gasped at the well-marked page in front of her.

"Why do you let people do that, Jesus," asked Rose in sincere respect for the sacred book.

"It's not a sin, Rose, honest," insisted Christ, looking at Pastor Ansel while they both fought the urge to laugh. "Rose, if it's done right, it helps you study. Put the ribbon of your Bible in that spot, and turn with Me to John 20:1."

> Early on the first day of the week, while it was still dark, Mary Magdalene went to the tomb and saw that the stone had been removed from the entrance.

"Where are you going with this, Lord?" asked Lloyd.

"It will all make sense. Just wait please, son. The best way to study scripture is by using other scripture. See what I've done to that passage in John, Rose? You do that. Stick another ribbon in John's gospel, and move over to Mark."

> When the Sabbath was over, Mary Magdalene, Mary the mother of James, and Salome bought spices so that they might go to anoint Jesus' body. Very early on the first day of the week, just after sunrise, they were on their way to the tomb and they asked each other, "Who will roll the stone away from the entrance of the tomb?" (Mark 16:1–3)

"Finally," said Jesus, "let's look at Luke."

> On the first day of the week, very early in the morning, the women took the spices they had prepared and went to the tomb. They found the stone rolled away from the tomb… (Luke 24:1–2)

"I'm beginning to see some things," Lloyd informed the others.

"What's that, Lloyd?" asked Pastor Ansel.

"There were several women at the tomb even though John mentions only Mary Magdalene. Mary was there 'while it was still dark.' The other gospels mention more than one woman," continued Lloyd. "Mark also mentions Mary Magdalene. It says that she arrived at the tomb 'just after sunrise.' She must have come back to the tomb a second time."

"Well done, Lloyd," praised Christ.

"Lord," said Pastor Ansel, "the Bible says in Matthew that there's a rumor among unsaved Jews—even today—that Your body was taken out of the tomb by Your apostles so they could claim you were resurrected. Some of those women believed You were resurrected because it says in chapter 28, verse 8 of Matthew that they were 'afraid yet filled with joy.'"

"You're right on both counts," Jesus smiled. "Can anyone tell me how I got out of the tomb?"

Pastor Ansel, Mary, Marcus, and the Peaces looked at each other mischievously and shouted, "Through the door!"

"No," said Christ, "the boulder was removed to let other people in."

"Is that so?" mused Rose.

"It sure is, honey. I came through the wall of the tomb."

"Lord, it says in the gospel of John that Peter and John didn't connect the empty tomb with your resurrection," said Pastor Ansel, carefully writing everything in Lydia's journal.

"You've got that right, Ansel. They initially thought, like Mary Magdalene, that someone had stolen My body."

Pastor Ansel then brought their attention to John 20:3–10.

> So Peter and the other disciple started for the tomb. Both were running, but the other disciple outran Peter and reached the tomb first. He bent over and looked in at the strips of linen lying there but did not go in. Then Simon Peter came along behind him and went straight into the tomb. He saw the strips of linen lying there, as well as the cloth that had been wrapped around Jesus' head. The cloth was still lying in its place, separate from the linen. Finally the other disciple, who had reached the tomb first, also went inside. He saw and believed. (They still did not understand from Scripture that Jesus had to rise from the dead.) Then the disciples went back to where they were staying.

"Lord," uttered Pastor Ansel, "if someone stole Your body like the unsaved Jews claim, how did they have time to fold your face cloth, leave it in a place separate from the burial shroud, and make their getaway?"

"Excellent point," answered Jesus. "I'm so glad you noticed that."

"How would it serve their purpose to steal Your dead body anyway?" said Pastor Ansel. "Your body would still be dead. The apostles wouldn't have wanted to prevent Your resurrection, and the skeptics wouldn't dare try again."

"I like the part where you appear to all Your apostles," Marcus suddenly spoke up.

"Read it, Marcus," commanded Jesus.

"I would be glad to," responded the soldier.

> Now as they said these things, Jesus Himself stood in the midst of them, and said to them, "Peace to you." But they were terrified and frightened, and supposed they had seen a spirit. And He said to them, "Why are you troubled? And why do doubts arise in your hearts? Behold My hands and My feet, that it is I Myself. Handle Me and see, for a spirit does not have flesh and bones as you see I have." (Luke 24:36–39, NKJV)

"Lord, where did Your spirit go between Your death and Your resurrection?" thought Lloyd out loud.

"I went to hell first for three reasons. One, I was full of everyone else's sin and therefore was unfit for heaven until I exchanged a mortal body for an immortal one. Two, I had to take back the keys of hell, which Satan stole from Me—"

"Excuse me, Lord, but why would you want the keys to hell?" pondered Lloyd.

"Jesus, can I answer that question?" asked Pastor Ansel.

Christ nodded.

"Lucifer, who is now Satan, took them when he fell from heaven. He's called the prince of this world in John 12:31 because Adam and Eve gave their dominion over to the devil when sin entered the earth."

"Satan offered to give them to Me if I would worship him," explained Christ.

"It makes far more sense for Jesus to have the keys anyway," exclaimed Pastor Ansel. "I shudder to think what would happen if the devil still had those keys."

"Who has dominion now that You've been resurrected?" voiced Lloyd.

"Yeshua has restored partial dominion to human beings on earth. But the earth will never have full dominion until the millennium," said Mary.

"Yeshua?" inquired Marcus.

"It's Hebrew. Jesus in Greek. Right, Mother?"

"His earthly family calls Him Yesh." Mary glowed.

"Lord, You mentioned that there was a third reason You went to hell," redirected Marcus.

"I had to prove that death and hell had no power over Me," taught Christ.

"Why do people on earth have only partial dominion?" asked Lloyd.

"When I originally gave Adam and Eve full dominion, they were perfect. They plunged themselves and the entire creation into utter cursed chaos."

"Yeshua doesn't completely trust fallen humanity," boomed the Father gently.

"You love the people on earth, right?" prodded Marcus.

"I sure do, especially the Church Militant," declared Jesus.

"But Abba just said—" Marcus began.

"He said I didn't completely trust them," reiterated Christ. "There's a big difference. Today the vast majority of the Church Militant has one foot in My kingdom and the other in the world."

"Where did You go when You left hell?" asked Lloyd.

"Prior to My resurrection, I was in a place called Hades. Half of it was where redeemed souls went awaiting My death and resurrection. I freed those people and brought them here to the third heaven. Once I saw to Timothy's comfort, I came down to earth, assumed My resurrected body, and met Mary Magdalene outside the garden tomb."

"Timothy, Paul's missionary companion?" pondered Rose.

"No," answered Jesus. "The one on my right when I was crucified."

"Lord, You mentioned in scripture that the tomb You used was in a garden. It couldn't have been in the Church of the Holy Sepulchre then," concluded Lloyd.

"You learn more of the Bible every day, Lloyd. I'm pleased…Let's turn to Luke 24, beginning with verse 40," instructed Jesus. "Would you please read from there? I've underlined what I want you to emphasize in My Bible."

> When He had said this, He showed them His hands and His feet. But while they still did not believe for joy, and marveled, He said to them, "Have you any food here?" So they gave Him a piece of a broiled fish and some honeycomb. And He took *it* and ate in their presence. (Luke 24:40–43, NKJV)

"Lord," said Pastor Ansel, "did You eat just because You were hungry?"

"No, I also wanted to show My apostles that a resurrected body is capable of consuming food."

"Lord," questioned Lloyd, "why did the apostles think You were a ghost on Your resurrection day?"

"Two reasons. First, even though they'd seen Me raise the dead, and I told them about My resurrection many times before My crucifixion, they were still consumed with grief because of My death until they saw Me. Second, the outline of the immortal body is not clearly defined even though it looks and feels like a real body in almost every other respect."

"Please explain 'almost,' Lord."

"We don't need to use a toilet," said Rose. "I'm not sure it was right to mention that, but you did ask, Pastor Almstedt."

"It's okay, Rose." chuckled Christ. "There are three other things that are different about the immortal body. There are no reproductive organs, the senses are keener, and you can breathe underwater."

"Jesus, please show me the dining room, where I can serve You and my other guests some food. I know now there's food, not just because of what You told us but because I'm hungry. What is there to eat?" asked Pastor Ansel.

"There's everything you can imagine," said Jesus.

"Here in heaven, there are also many things not found on earth," boomed the Heavenly Father gently.

"May you please name one?" Pastor Ansel requested of the Lord.

"Manna," replied Jesus. "We can have them as hors d'oeuvres."

Pastor Ansel decided that the main course he and his company would have was steaks with baked potatoes and asparagus. Rose and Lloyd had brought banana cream pie, which they had for dessert. Angels prepared most of the meal, but Rose and Mary insisted on helping with the preparations. Lunch was served in the dining room amidst conversation about the Chinese Baptist Fellowship, after Jesus said the blessing at Pastor Ansel's suggestion.

Christ commented on how much He loved the Chinese people.

Pastor Ansel asked the Lord, "What if I could meet some of the Chinese who are in heaven and had family currently worshiping in the Friend of Sinners Baptist Church building every Sunday afternoon?"

Christ said, "That sounds like a wonderful idea! I'll come with You. I have gifts from one of the storehouses for all of them."

"Is it a Chinese holiday?" inquired Rose.

"No," answered Jesus.

"Yesh is impressed by their bravery," Mary explained. "He's also answering the prayers of their families by giving each one gifts that their family on earth isn't able to give them right now."

Pastor Ansel told Lloyd, "My son Alex is an artist."

"I'd like to see his work sometime," replied Lloyd.

"I'm sure you'll have that opportunity in due time," said Christ. "One of reasons I wanted you here, Ansel, was so you could help Me prepare a place for Lydia."

"Please, Lord," uttered a suddenly startled Pastor Ansel, "don't take her now. My sons and Grace need her."

"They will have her for quite a while, according to earth time. But I believe in being organized."

"Jesus, while we're on the subject of being organized, I need time to prepare tomorrow's lesson for those pastors."

"There's plenty of time for that, son."

"Why are we feeding them from the gospel John?" asked Pastor Ansel.

"'I fed you with milk, not solid food, for you were not ready for it. And even now you are not yet ready'" quoted Jesus.

"Shouldn't they be eating spiritual meat by now?" asked Pastor Ansel.

"Yes, that's true. My plan is for you to help Me mold them," stated the Lord, taking His last bite of steak.

"Were any of them sanctified on earth?" inquired Pastor Ansel.

"They've done some good works, but usually not at my bidding. They've taught their congregations all the comfortable Scriptures while neglecting the harsh ones. They've asked me to be their Savior so they can have salvation. I want everyone who claims to know Me as their personal Savior to bear fruit through obedience. Satan and his demons know Me too, but they don't obey Me willingly."

"Do the pastors whom Pastor Ansel will be teaching love people?" wondered Rose out loud.

"Yes, Rose. In a way," Lloyd responded. "Pastors, like parents, have to balance tough love with tenderness."

"Pastors who don't, on the other hand, love their congregations right into hell," interjected Jesus.

"That's terrible!" fumed Pastor Ansel. "What you've just described is not the church. It's a religious club."

"Right. Well said," answered Christ with a smile. He put a reassuring hand on Pastor Ansel's shoulder then turned to the rest of their party and said, "Rose, Lloyd, Mother, and Marcus, I need to be alone with Pastor Ansel for a little while. So if the four of you could please excuse yourselves for a bit, I would appreciate it."

His other guests left with promises to have Pastor Ansel over to their place; then the Lord turned to Pastor Ansel and said, "It's time for your review.

3

The Review

They walked back to the media center in Pastor Ansel's mansion. Instantly before him was every day of his life on earth. In each case, he was able to see and feel the effects of his righteous deeds and sins on people in his life.

"You were a wonderful pastor, Ansel, even more now that you're here. You were also a wonderful husband and father. And I'm sure Lilly would want Me to tell you that you're a great friend too."

"Did you mean what you said about my being a good husband and father?" Pastor Ansel heard himself say.

"I sure did. John and Alex are two fine young men. You were in large part responsible for that."

"Thanks, Lord, but we had help all along the way."

"Lydia adored you. Still does."

Soon after it began, the review was over. Jesus left Pastor Ansel with the Holy Spirit to prepare for his lesson. Pastor Ansel wondered where his student pastors had gone wrong spiritually. He hated to start with the salvation prayer since, according to the Lord, they'd already said it, the proof being that they would be there tomorrow.

But with the probability that the rest of their understanding of regeneration (entrance of the Holy Spirit into someone who wants to receive Jesus as their Savior) and sanctification (the outcome on the believer of his good works done in accordance with the will and for the glory of Christ) were done for a less-than-perfect reason, Pastor Ansel saw no other alternative but to start with the reason behind each one's request for salvation. Pastor Ansel wondered about the three clergymen with wrong assumptions about hell. *Wouldn't being in heaven because of the presence of the Holy Spirit automatically change their view of that?*

He no sooner had let the thought pass from his mind than the Holy Spirit said, "Those three are going back to earth."

He began with John 3, Christ's conversation with Nicodemus. He wanted to meet Jesus because God was with Him. Christ wanted him to understand that, like the wind, so it was with the Holy Spirit. "Nicodemus confused physical birth with spiritual birth," wrote Pastor Ansel.

He would meet with each one privately. That way they wouldn't feel intimidated. *It would be helpful*, he thought, *for each of my colleagues to begin by giving their personal testimony. Dealing with the issue of sin would be next.*

In this postmodern era, wherein a lot of people thought it didn't matter, it was unavoidable. Pastor Ansel typed the following verses on his laptop:

> If we say that we have no sin, we deceive ourselves, and the truth is not in us. If we confess our sins, he is faithful and just to forgive us our sins, and to cleanse us from all unrighteousness. If we say that we have not sinned, we make him a liar, and his word is not in us. (1 John 1:8–10, KJV)

Next, the Holy Spirit led Pastor Ansel to John 3:16–18. He knew that Christians and most unbelievers knew that verse by heart, but not the way the Holy Spirit was asking him to write it. He quickly typed the words:

> For God so loved the world, that he gave his one and only Son, that *whoever believes in Him shall not perish* but have eternal life. For God did not send his Son into the world to condemn the world, but to save the world through him. Whoever believes in him is not condemned, but *whoever does not believe stands condemned already* because they have not believed in the name of God's one and only Son.

"Is there anything else You want to be included in this lesson?" wrote Pastor Ansel in an e-mail to Christ. He attached a copy of what he had written.

Jesus's answer came within a few seconds. "Looks great so far. Tell them something they already know."

"Take delight in the Lord, and he will give you the desires of your heart," Pastor Ansel typed.

Prompted by the Holy Spirit, he sent the slightly revised copy to the Lord for His approval. Within seconds, Jesus appeared beside him.

"Well done, Ansel."

"Are you sure there isn't more I can do?" asked Pastor Ansel.

"No. The lesson is complete," said Jesus, looking at His copy with pleasure.

"May I ask why You wanted that Psalm verse cited?" asked Pastor Ansel.

"Ansel, a few of those pastors I'm having you reeducate care more about what their congregation thinks than what I think. That's got to stop."

4

Tour of Heaven

"**W**ould you like to see more of this mansion or explore the outdoors? You've been inside since you've arrived."

"Let's go outside. My mansion will be here when the tour of heaven is over," assessed Pastor Ansel, following Jesus out the door of his home.

"Master," Herman whispered loudly, looking joyfully at Pastor Ansel, "there's something important you need to know. Jesus should tell you about your desks, but He's humble."

"Don't call me master, Herman!" said Pastor Ansel angrily. "Only the Trinity can be worshiped. If telling me this would make Christ less humble, then it's better left unsaid."

"Herman wasn't usurping My authority," said Christ. "He knows his place."

"I do. Thank You, Yeshua, my God," said the wounded angel, turning his face abruptly away from Pastor Ansel.

"My Father," said Jesus, "please let Herman tell Pastor Ansel about his desks before he busts."

The Heavenly Father roared with laughter. "Herman, you need to realize that Pastor Ansel just didn't want to sin."

"All right, precious God," said Herman, the light returning to his eyes.

"Jesus and Joseph made your desks by hand," the angel whispered loudly.

"Really? That's incredible! Thank You very much. I want to thank Joseph, Lord."

"You could just speak them into existence."

"Lord, why have you given me so much?"

"You haven't seen everything I've given you yet."

"I don't mean salvation," explained Pastor Ansel. "I received You as my Savior, so a relationship with You and eternal life were expected.

Jesus listened as though Pastor Almstedt was the only one in heaven.

"When You were on earth, you loved Me for who I was, not for what I could give you," said Christ.

"I brought you another friend." Jesus smiled.

Just then Pastor Ansel heard a familiar bark.

"Bear!" Disappointment momentarily washed over Pastor Ansel. "He died on earth."

"Yes," Christ responded gently.

"Lord, You recreated Bear for me!"

"Remember what I said when you asked me how I got a photo of you and your family Lydia for Lloyd?"

"Yes, You quoted Luke 1:37, where it says, 'For nothing will be impossible with God.' You also said that You could work miracles, so getting a photo for Lloyd was, surely, no problem."

"Right," agreed Jesus. "Let's take this miracle for a walk."

"Herman"— Jesus laughed—"there's no way you could've known about those desks unless you were snooping around Joseph's woodshop again."

"Lord, there's your friend Peter," said Bear.

"Jesus, Bear just *spoke* to you! Is that an example of your sense of humor, or can all the animals here talk?"

"Every animal in heaven can communicate with either sound or words. Once, every animal on earth could speak before the fall and afterward."

"Jesus, the only biblical evidence of animals talking before the fall was a snake that Satan possessed."

"You're right," said Christ. "Satan copied Me. I didn't see a need to write about animals talking before the fall, except in the temptation of Adam and Eve. But the Holy Spirit can land on an animal and cause them to speak. Satan tempted Adam and Eve for the same reason he tempted Me. My

Father wanted to see if they would accept His sovereign will. There was actually nothing wrong with that fruit."

"Oh, I know." grinned Pastor Ansel.

"I'm more upset with Adam than I am with Eve," sighed Herman. "Husbands are supposed to protect their wives. When Eve was being tempted, Adam was silent. When he finally did speak, it was to blame Eve."

Pastor Ansel removed his sandals. The grass was long (each blade was perhaps one inch tall). It felt like fine velvet against his feet. The Holy Spirit was emanating through the grass.

"Lord, about the woodshop…I just wanted to be with You and happened to see them," confessed Herman, relieved that the Lord wasn't angry.

"Lord," blurted Pastor Ansel, "I've never seen so many beautiful colors! There's even some that aren't on earth."

"Herman, forgive Adam and Eve, please. Righteous anger is okay even here, but don't let it become a grudge. Holding grudges is like drinking poison yourself and intensely expecting the person you don't like to die from it," insisted Christ.

"Ok, Sire," sighed Herman.

He then looked at Pastor Ansel and asked, "Pastor Ansel, are we friends?"

"We sure are! Especially because you were so kind to the Lord in His hour of need."

"Look, Jesus, the streets are really gold!" Pastor Ansel cried with an innocence that clearly delighted the Lord. "I can see myself. They're so transparent!"

Pastor Ansel knelt down so he could touch the smooth, hard surface with his hand. Bear was done resting and pulled insistently at his leash till he was standing next to the apostle Peter.

"Hi, pal." Peter rubbed the dog behind the ears.

"Have you been a good been a good boy for Pastor Ansel?" inquired the short, burly fisherman-turned-disciple.

Peter's shoulder-length hair was dishwater blond. It was unkempt but clean. It seemed longer at the hairline than those of most people Pastor Ansel knew. He had blue-gray eyes and a long, bulbous nose and a narrow-but-bright smile that seemed to cover the entire width of his face. He had a long face with a long, seemingly huge jawline and a large, square chin. He stood 5'8" tall and wore a white tunic with a yellow sash.

Pastor Ansel had been so focused on Peter and the Book of Life that for a few minutes, he didn't notice that Bear had turned his head so he could face Pastor Ansel. Rifling through the book, the apostle found the entry that both men sought: "Almstedt, Philip, Ansel Rev."

"Feel better now, Ansel? You looked concerned," observed the key bearer. "Names in this book are listed in alphabetical order, by family."

"Well, am I good?" asked the shar-pei, giving Pastor Ansel a pleading glance.

Peter and Pastor Ansel laughed long and hard at Bear's expression.

"Yes, you're good," answered Pastor Ansel.

Behind Peter were the four east gates, each made of one enormous pearl. Four tall angels guarded them from the outside.

"We've talked business. Now I say we have some fun," said Peter. "Let's go…"

"Bear, stop!" shouted Pastor Ansel, as the dog suddenly started running toward the west gates.

"Is this what you're after, boy?" asked Christ, holding a tiny cat. "He rescued her from traffic, Ansel."

Bear assumed a submissive position in front of Jesus.

"Good boy, Bear," the Lord praised, stroking the dog's back.

"I'm sorry, Jesus," exhaled Pastor Ansel. "He could get out of hand on earth. I should've guessed our perspective would be different here, even for my dog."

"'The wolf also shall dwell with the lamb, and the leopard shall lie down with the kid; and the calf and the young lion and the fatling together; and a little child shall lead them. And the cow and the bear shall feed; their young ones shall lie down together: and the lion shall eat straw like the ox,'" quoted Christ.

Pastor Ansel squatted so he could look into Bear's eyes. "Sorry, buddy. I didn't know that you were just being a good friend."

Bear barked, encouraging his new pal to follow him back to Pastor Ansel's mansion. Jesus handed the cat to Pastor Ansel, who reluctantly agreed to give her a place to live until Lilly came to heaven and claimed her. Pastor Ansel examined the tiny creature with curiosity and affection. He hadn't noticed the gray patch on its back at first. Christ told him that the cat was a female who liked the humans in heaven and was younger than she had been on earth.

"Herman!" called Pastor Ansel. "Take Bear and"—Pastor Ansel looked at the little tag on her collar, which was engraved with the name Mia—"Take these two home, please."

"Sure will. I'll ask Selah and Gloria to help me, if that's all right with you, Pastor Ansel. Pets have guardian angels too." smiled Herman. "Selah has charge of Bear, and Gloria looks after Mia."

"Put her on my back, Ansel," said Bear happily.

"Okay. But she's a lot smaller than you. Be careful with her, Bear. She's not a toy."

5

The Fishing Trip

Pastor Ansel walked slowly back to the east gate, wanting to continue his conversation with Peter. He grinned, watching his two well-guarded friends as he went. Suddenly Jesus appeared.

"Peter, you said you wanted to go somewhere with me?"

"Lord," said Peter, "if it's all right with You, the other apostles and I would like to take You and Pastor Ansel fishing."

"He wants Me to tag along so they can get more fish." Jesus laughed.

"Lord, Scripture makes it clear from these verses that nothing dies. Aren't we allowed to eat our catch?"

"We fish in the second heaven all the time." Peter grinned.

"When the Bible speaks of God making the heavens… it means there are three levels," said Christ to Pastor Ansel.

"Right below the third heaven, where we live, is the second heaven. It's a beautiful area but not like here. We hunt and fish in the upper half of this region. Satan sometimes wanders around in there, but don't worry about having to deal with spiritual warfare tonight. You're a member of the glorified church now. We'll fight during Armageddon, but that's still a long way off. Let's worship, rest, and have fun until then."

"Lord, what's in the lower part of the second heaven?"

"Planet galaxies," replied Jesus.

"Where is the first heaven?" asked a child who had been innocently listening.

She wore a white dress tied with a light-blue ribbon in the middle. Her hair was dark, long, and curly. She had olive skin, dark-brown eyes, and a beautiful smile.

"Judith," said the Lord, "the first heaven can be seen from earth. It's placed where the airplanes, kites, and birds fly."

"Oh, the sky!" she said joyfully.

"Yes, that's right," said Jesus, kneeling on the ground in order to look her in the face and plant a tender kiss on her forehead.

"I asked the Holy Spirit if I could hear what You and your friends were saying," confessed Judith.

"Hi, Judith," said Pastor Ansel.

"Hello, my friend," Peter said to the child.

After the short greetings, Judith skipped off to play.

"Peter, what kind of fish does heaven have?" asked Pastor Ansel.

"Heaven is a lot like Israel," interjected Jesus. "Israel has three native species of fish. Sardines, Barbels, and Musht." (Musht, Pastor Ansel discovered later in his library, was also called St. Peter's fish but is more widely known as tilapia.)

"Peter, there are some things I want to show Pastor Ansel before we fish," remarked Christ.

6

Revelation of Heaven

"Look, the jewel wall mentioned in Revelation 21!" exclaimed Pastor Ansel in amazement. He looked with great interest and awe at each row of beautiful gems. Each one had a tiny plaque with the apostle's name engraved on it.

"Wow…Lydia, read that chapter to me. I never imagined anything like this!"

Then something else caught Pastor Ansel's eye.

"What a beautiful garden!" declared Pastor Ansel.

"That's Lilly Peace's estate and her roses. I'm sure Lilly wouldn't mind if you picked some for Lydia."

"These yellow ones are nice," observed Pastor Ansel. "Are you sure Lilly won't mind?"

"Positive," answered Jesus. "She's a friend, and besides, I can grow them again in a matter of seconds."

"Cut the stems long," suggested the Lord. "They're prettier that way."

"Okay, but Lydia won't be coming for years yet."

"Nothing dies here," Christ reminded him.

"Where is Lydia's mansion?" asked Pastor Ansel.

"Next to yours, on the right. You can put the flowers there now if you like. There's a large crystal vase with a matching ribbon already inside."

"You think of everything." Pastor Ansel smiled. "Would it be all right if I went in Lilly's mansion and left her a thank-you note for the roses?"

"Sure," said Jesus. "I'll wait here for you."

—◯—

Inside Lilly's mansion, Pastor Ansel found a corner desk with post-it notes on it. He wrote,

Dear Lilly,

Took some roses from your beautiful garden for Lydia. Jesus assures me that you won't mind.

Looking forward to seeing you when you get here. With much love,

Your friend,
Pastor Ansel Almstedt

———◈———

Pastor Ansel rejoined the Lord outside.

"Where do we meet for corporate worship?"

"Everyone in heaven meets in the throne room," informed Christ. "There's also the Silver Palace. I'll take you there, but first there are some things I'd like to show you. Let's go to the field of white stones."

They arrived there in the blink of an eye.

"Here is your stone," said the Lord. "It has your spiritual name on it. No one will know that name except you and me. I'll only use that name for you when we're alone."

Pastor Ansel looked at the name and felt a rush of joy. It fit him to a T. Engraved on the stone was a name that described the unique and spiritually intimate relationship that a person had with the Lord. It was also symbolic of acquittal. They lingered a long while in the field.

Christ envisioned them back in the city. When they got there, they stood in front of what appeared to be an office building.

"Jesus, I'd rather be outside."

"I know, son, but you're going to want to see this."

Inside a backroom, in what looked to Pastor Ansel like China cabinets, were glass bottles filled with tears. There were glass bottles for each member of Pastor Almstedt's family.

"Why don't we go swimming?" suggested Christ.

"Where do we go? The only lake I know of mentioned in Scripture is the lake of fire in hell," said Pastor Ansel. "Also, I don't have swimming trunks."

"I was talking about the River of Life."

"Sounds great," said Pastor Ansel.

"You can swim in your robes."

"No, I wouldn't want to do that. It would ruin my robes, and it would be too constricting to swim in them. I don't have a towel either."

Jesus and Pastor Ansel imagined themselves by the River of Life. They were instantly there.

"Tell you what," Jesus began. "You jump in, and if you feel uncomfortable, I can give you a swimming suit. You won't need a towel."

Pastor Ansel was astonished that they could carry on a conversation underwater. There were many species of fish, including walleye, sunfish, and all the other ones that Peter had previously spoken about. The plant life also reflected God's brilliance and glory.

When they stepped out of the water, their clothes were dry and soft. Poised at either end of the steady stream of humanity and wildlife were angels directing traffic.

The Throne Room

"Here we are," the Lord announced.

Directly in front of them was the throne room.

"Clear the way! Jesus is here!" exclaimed the Angel Gabriel.

"Hello, Pastor Ansel. We've been waiting for you," bubbled Gabriel joyfully. He then resumed his place to the left of Jesus.

Inside, Pastor Ansel saw the prophetess Anna, who as on earth was in a perpetual state of worship, waiting to see her Messiah.

Pastor Ansel knelt down and kissed the Lord's wounds.

"Isn't He wonderful?" said Anna in a loud whisper.

"He sure is," agreed Pastor Ansel, quietly.

Suddenly, Pastor Ansel recognized a familiar biblical figure.

"Is that...? It is!" said Pastor Ansel, finding it hard to keep his voice low. He hung back till the servant of the King finished his prayer.

"King David."

"The one and only," said King David. He stood a couple inches shorter than the Lord. He had a round cut to his auburn hair and a round face with hazel eyes. He was lanky. His nose was average in length, slightly pointed. His comely face had a wide grin. He threw his gold crown at the feet of Jesus. Pastor Ansel, as though on cue, did the same.

"Jesus, can I...?" began Pastor Ansel.

"Go ahead and say hello," said Jesus.

Pastor Ansel greeted both Gabriel and David.

Christ walked over to Mary and asked, "Is Joseph available?"

"Did I hear my name?" asked Joseph, appearing in the throne room.

"Yes. Pastor Ansel just wanted to thank you for helping Me with the desks."

"No thanks are necessary. Just enjoy them. That will be thanks enough."

"Who is the little guy?" asked Pastor Ansel.

"Brian, son of Willard," said King David.

"He's Lilly's younger brother," said Jesus.

"Hi, Brian," whispered Pastor Ansel. "Hello, again Rose."

"Lord, would You join us for supper tonight?" inquired Rose.

"Leftovers aren't good enough for the Son of God? Is that why you've waited so long to share a meal with Me?"

"David, wanna see my truck?" Brian blurted suddenly, forgetting his volume.

"Brian, go over there and play while I talk to the Lord," said Rose quietly. "Leave King David alone. He's praying."

"I like leftovers, Rose."

"Is that so?" mused Rose.

"It is. Tell you what, Rose, let My men and I bring our catch over to your boarding house. Pastor Almstedt is coming too. Angels will serve and clean up just like they did this afternoon when we visited Pastor Ansel."

"Fine. Are kids invited?"

"You and I love children. Right, Rose?"

"Yes."

"'Suffer little children, and forbid them not, to come unto me: for of such is the kingdom of heaven,'" quoted Christ.

"I love Brian and that verse," admitted Rose. "I just wish he wasn't so hyper."

"Turn that wish into a prayer, and I'll see what I can do."

—ᴡᴡ—

Pastor Ansel resumed writing to his beloved Lydia.

8

A Human Catch

We caught musht and barbells and sardines in the second heaven. Exactly like the ones in the River of Life. Sardines were the fish used at the feeding of the five thousand. (The sardines are not like the ones found in tiny cans in grocery stores in America.)

Christ put some American fish in there too so it would be more enjoyable for me. I caught three enormous Alaskan salmon, two walleye, and six sardines. Jesus told me that Lilly likes walleye. He said that I should have her over for lunch when she comes and share one with her. But the biggest catch of the day was not fish but *friends*. Each of the apostles is unique and special.

Ever since Pentecost, brash Peter has gentled, according to the Lord—especially around the children. He's still a take charge kind of guy, and he preaches better than any of them.

James and John, as you'll recall, Lydia, were given to fits of anger on earth. Jesus called them *Boanerges* or "sons of thunder." The brothers are no longer vying for a seat next to Christ's throne. They are now as gentle as lambs though stirred by righteous anger every so often. Now they're content to have whatever God has for them.

James is intelligent and warmhearted but doesn't wear his emotions on his sleeve the way John does. James was martyred in Jerusalem.

Lydia, John's love is something of tremendous beauty, only surpassed by the Lord's love for him. He is more like Christ than any of the other apostles. He refers to himself as the one whom Jesus loved.

Andrew is very reserved. He's like John to the extent that he loves deeply. Andrew has won more souls to Christ than any apostle, except Paul. He was the first disciple to recognize Jesus as the Messiah.

Philip is a curious extravert. Prayer was difficult for him on earth before Pentecost because he had to quiet himself without the Holy Spirit. Philip was the first evangelist to the Gentiles. His name means horse lover. Philip was fiercely practical—so much so that it would often interfere with his faith unlike Andrew, who was very resourceful.

Thomas is a clearheaded, analytical man of courage and intellect. He was one of the only ones willing to die with our Lord, Lydia.

Matthew used to be a thief, but now he's a giver. In addition to giving the world a beautiful gospel of the Lord's kingship that bears his name, he gives away his possessions, and he gives of his time. He learned from the Lord to treat each person like they were the only person on earth. He does no less in heaven. Matthew's name means "God's gift."

Nathaniel is the Israelite in whom there is no guile, according to Jesus.

Christ is always right. He's as honest as a day in heaven is long, Lydia. Now I believe it not just because Christ says it in the Bible. I know him. His name means "God has given."

James, the son of Alphaeus, is good with numbers. He either picked that up directly from Christ or from his brother, the apostle Matthew. He likes to laugh and have fun. Lydia, I can hardly wait for James to meet our friend from church Eric Dunn.

Judas Thaddeus was a zealot on earth, but unlike Judas Iscariot, he didn't give up on Christ and willingly hand himself over to the devil. Initially his sole objective in life was to overthrow the Roman empire; then he met Jesus and learned that the Lord's purpose in coming to earth was regeneration of every human soul. There are many Romans here (besides Marcus, who I've spoken of before), and Thaddeus loves them all, which just goes to show you what time spent with Jesus can accomplish.

He plays the harp and the recorder. He brought his recorder on our fishing trip, Lydia. It's not something I'd normally advise on earth, but here it doesn't scare the fish away. Jesus sang to the melody that Thaddeus played. It brought to mind that verse in Zephaniah 3:17 (NKJV) that says, "He will rejoice over you with gladness… He will rejoice over you with singing." (Jesus has a beautiful baritone voice, by the way.)

9

Angelic Warfare and Worship

Suddenly, Michael the archangel appeared and whispered in the Lord's ear.

"Michael, you gather a legion of the heavenly host and surround him, understand?"

"Satan is here," said Jesus calmly. "Don't worry. He's only here to kill our catch, unless you wanted to eat live fish?"

"Couldn't You kill the fish without him, the way You did that fruitless fig tree in the Bible?" asked Pastor Ansel. "I really don't enjoy the idea of having to see the creature who's the source of all evil in the universe."

"You want Me to get glory, right?"

"Yes."

Pastor Ansel studied the wide range of emotion that crossed the Lord's face: there was anger, joy, mischief, and something he couldn't quite identify.

"Stand back and watch while I receive all the glory, fellas. Don't worry. None of you will suffer. I know you've entered your eternal rest. Take it away, Michael!"

Pastor Ansel's glorified eyes could suddenly make out not only the whole legion that had encircled and blinded their prey but also the adversary being pinned to the ground by the neck with the tip of the archangel's sword. Pastor Ansel saw the third heaven open above them, and the entire company of heaven erupted in thunderous applause as Jesus gestured broadly toward the spectacle at the legion's center.

"Well done, Michael!" exclaimed the grateful Lord.

———

Back in the third heaven, Pastor Ansel joined worship in the Silver Palace. He was surprised at how well he could sing. He was able to understand each song—even though they were sung in all of earth's languages and some that were only in heaven. Jesus sang a solo about His love for the church. The music was in more than four parts.

Martin Luther preached a sermon on Romans 8:1, 35.

> There is now no condemnation for those who are in Christ Jesus…Who shall separate us from the love of Christ? Shall trouble or hardship or persecution or famine or nakedness or danger or sword?

Luther added parts of his testimony in the sermon since careful examination of those verses began his journey toward Christ. The last hymn was "Alleluia! Sing to Jesus"; then the whole glorified church lifted the Lord up on their shoulders and marched around the Silver Palace.

10

Family Festivities at the Boarding House

After the service, Pastor Ansel rejoined Jesus at Rose and Lloyd's boarding house. There was no need for money in heaven: everything in heaven was free. During the Millennium, anyone who was given a job in heaven could spend what they received at that time; they each had their own estate.

Rose and Lloyd's boarding house was a moneymaking venture. (Just as well since they loved to entertain.)

"Pastor Ansel, this is our daughter Louise," said Lloyd, seeing her come through the wall. "The family calls her Lulu."

"Hi, honey," said Lloyd. "Sit down if you like, and have some supper. There's plenty."

"Okay, Daddy. Hello, Mother," said Lulu, kissing both her parents. She also hugged Jesus and greeted each of the apostles. She stood 5'6" tall, had a flat flip cut to her dark-brown hair. Her bangs hid most of her fair oval forehead.

"Lilly's aunt," observed the apostle John, whose place card on the table was next to Christ's.

"Father, thank You for this food, the people gathered here, and, most of all, our beautiful Savior, without whom humanity would be in hell," prayed Lloyd at the Lord's request.

The apostles had gone on ahead after the service and put the fillet in the smokehouse. Gwen, Rose's sister, made her Owen's special homegrown carrots and boiled potatoes.

"Brian, eat your food, and stop playing with it!" scolded Lloyd. Turning to Pastor Ansel, he said, "Pastor Almstedt, I'd like to ask you a question. You're welcome to consider yourself part of this family—at least until Lydia and your sons come home. Is that agreeable to you? You don't have to answer right away. I've been given permission by everyone in the Peace family that's any relation to me to ask this."

After supper ended, Christ said, "Rose, I want to show you what the apostles and I do with leftovers. Get your Bible, and turn to Matthew 14:13–20."

"Are You gonna make me mark it up?"

"No, not if you don't want to. Read verse 20."

"'And they did all eat, and were filled: and they took up of the fragments that remained, twelve baskets full.'"

When Rose realized where Jesus was headed with this, she said with a smile, "I don't waste anything. I learned that during the Great Depression and World War II."

She then turned to her other guests and asked, "Would anybody like to take some leftovers home?"

They all readily agreed they would take some.

"Brian, take one bite of everything. Then you can leave the table. No ice cream for you though," said Lloyd.

"What's the d—dep—?" stammered his grandson.

"Depression," said Lloyd. "It was a time in America when most people went hungry."

"Dish up that ice cream, Rose. Brian wants to eat his whole meal," said Jesus.

"Grandma, can we invite Isaiah Jones to eat with us?"

"Yes, that's fine."

"Isaiah," Brian called out with unabated joy, "you can eat with us!"

"Isaiah is from a place where nobody ever had enough food," said Brian to Pastor Ansel.

"That's really nice that you invite him over to eat," said Pastor Ansel.

"Grandma, that's not enough," protested Brian, looking at Isaiah's plate.

"Isaiah, do you want more?" asked Rose in amazement.

"Oh no, ma'am. My plate's heaped full. Thank you for caring about me, precious white brother. Never gonna go hungry here though," declared the older child, giving Brian a high five.

Rose gave Isaiah a hug.

"How old are you, Isaiah?" asked Gwen.

"Just turned eight yesterday, ma'am."

He was politeness personified, observed Gwen. He stood 4'3" tall. His African-style hair was flat on top, with only the slightest hint of a wave on either side. He had a low forehead; small, round checks; a short, almost-square jawline; a long, narrow smile; and small, round chin.

"Now see here, Isaiah. I'm Rose and this is my sister, Gwen."

"Isaiah, everyone in heaven is family," Lloyd chimed in.

"Isaiah," queried Pastor Ansel, "does the Peace family treat you well?"

"They sure do," said Isaiah emphatically.

With that reply, Pastor Ansel knew what to do about Lloyd's offer.

"Provided it's temporary—like you said earlier—with one other condition, I accept your offer."

"What might that be?" pondered Lloyd out loud.

"I insist on keeping my last name," said Pastor Ansel.

"Of course." Lloyd smiled. "Changing your last name never occurred to me when I asked."

"Isaiah, do you wanna see my truck?" chirped Brian, swallowing his last spoonful of ice cream.

"We dance every night after supper for heaven's festival and for fun," Rose told Pastor Ansel.

"You're welcome to stay and watch or to join us," offered Lloyd to Pastor Ansel and Isaiah.

"Is the Baptist Church still opposed to dancing?" asked Lloyd as he watched his grandson and Isaiah playing with the toy truck on the braided rug just inside their door.

"Some people in the Baptist Church might still oppose it, but the Lord and Pastor Ansel don't," explained Jesus, slightly annoyed at the idea that anyone disliked it.

"I danced at the temple when I was twelve."

Rose answered the door as the doorbell rang.

"Boys, please move away from the door," Lulu instructed.

"Hi, David!" greeted both of the children when they saw their latest visitor.

Brian clapped, unable to contain himself at the sight of Israel's second greatest king.

"Hello, boys. Brian, I wanted to thank you for letting me finish my prayer when I was in the throne room before. Now I can see that truck you wanted to show me."

"Ansel, he'd like you to see it too," remarked Christ.

"Wow, a red one! Looks just like the one I had on earth."

"Could ja get in and drive it?" asked Brian, his eyes getting as big as saucers at the thought.

"Yeah, I sure could." Pastor Ansel laughed tenderly, pulling at his chin.

"It's a wonderful truck, Brian," said David, becoming as animated as the blond youngster. "I have some horses, boys. "Would either of you like to go riding with me?"

"Jesus has a horse too," explained Brian with the same wide-eyed look he had about Pastor Ansel's truck.

"King David, I'll go riding with you!" Isaiah piped up.

"Me too!" echoed Brian joyfully.

Rose had been showing Pastor Ansel family photos; and each person she mentioned, as well as several others, streamed into the boarding house to dance. Everyone brought their ethnic costumes, a different one for each dance.

"Grandpa, can I call Ari?" asked Brian.

"Yes, but hurry, Brian. We're about ready to start."

"Oh, that reminds me!" said Gwen. "Isaiah, I have something for you. Come with me."

She led him into a backroom. She handed him a beautifully gift wrapped box. He tore it open like only a child would.

"A Ugandan costume!" said Isaiah with genuine delight. "Oh, Miss Gwen, thank you!"

They joined the crowd just as Lloyd was explaining the first dance.

"The Hora, in honor of Christ. It's been the national dance of Israel since 1924, usually danced at weddings and bar and bat mitzvahs."

"Everybody, form a circle, hold hands," continued Lloyd, "and step forward toward the right with the left foot then follow with the right foot. Then bring the left foot back, followed by the right foot. Do this while holding hands and circling together in a fast and cheerful motion to the right. Large groups like ours allow for the creation of several concentric circles."

"Grandma, what does that big C word mean?" asked Brian.

Rose explained, "It's a circle inside another circle in this dance."

"Just let the Holy Spirit move your feet, honey," said Gwen.

Jesus insisted there be a short social break between dances.

"King David, did your grandma come to the dance?" asked an exuberant Brian.

"She sure did!" answered the boy's companion. "We danced right next to each other."

"Hello, Miss Ruth," called Brian and the crowd of children around him to David's ancestor.

"Hello, Queen Esther!" said the kids.

Pastor Ansel regarded the two women, and as he did, he couldn't help but compare them with each other and to his Lydia. Both had regal bearing though only one was royal on earth. Ruth stood about 5'7". She had a very slender build. Her hair was light brown and thinner than Lydia's. Pastor Ansel could see from King David's grandmother where the Lord got His beautiful green eyes. Lydia's eyes were blue. Lydia had a larger eye frame than Ruth. Both had an oval face. Ruth had a long, narrow nose, which, like Mary's, came to a graceful point. Lydia had a wide smile. Pastor Ansel missed her, but he wasn't sad.

"I bet you had lots of friends in school," probed Rose.

"Yes, but there were some who insisted on hating me because I was different."

"You mean," said Pastor Ansel, "because Joseph was not your biological father?"

"They would call Me *mamzer*, which translated means 'son of a prostitute,'" said Jesus. "The closest English word would be *bastard*."

"You told them 'I love you,'" guessed Pastor Ansel.

"Yes," answered Jesus. "Then I took them home to meet my mother so they could see who she really was...There was that and when My Father finally told Me one day in prayer that I was the Messiah.

"My brothers were so jealous— each of them but James and Jude, who was still a baby. They used the rope-and-pulley system Joseph had rigged up in the woodshop for carrying heavy objects to hang Me."

"Not by the neck?" exclaimed Rose in horror.

"No," said Mary. "They stretched out His arms with the rope, hastily made a cross, and attempted to hang Him on it."

"Where were you and Joseph when all this was going on?" replied Pastor Ansel, trying not to sound accusatory.

"My Father sent Joseph to My rescue. Joseph scolded Me after he got Me down for telling them I was the Messiah. Joses, Levi, and Simeon got whacked across their backsides with a board that had been used to make My "cross." They were sent to bed without supper. Mother was feeding Jude."

Lydia's Mansion

"I thought we could work on Lydia's mansion after things are finished here," suggested Christ, changing the topic.

"I got these curtains from one of the storehouses," said Rose.

"They do look nice," admitted Pastor Ansel. "But Lydia would say—"

"White symbolizes purity here," interrupted Jesus. "It doesn't collect dirt or grease."

"Okay, hang them in one of the kitchens." He smiled.

"I thought these candles would be nice in one of the bathrooms," said Mary, referring to those in Lydia's mansion.

Mary showed Pastor Ansel wallpaper with a vine motif, wherein the ends of each branch were artistically covered with a cluster of grapes.

"Rose, didn't you tell me over at my place that no one in heaven needs a toilet?" asked Pastor Ansel.

"Yes, that's so," answered Rose. "Our new bodies don't need food or soap and water," explained Rose.

"Except on rare occasions when a visitor needs to be scared straight," commented Lloyd, unable to resist raising his eyebrows in Christ's direction.

"We usually eat and bathe here just for enjoyment," said Jesus.

"You can put them in all the bathrooms." Pastor Ansel laughed.

"What about the chapel?" said Jesus. "Should we put flowers or candles in there? Or both?"

"I'm taking a risk when I say this," Pastor Ansel confessed, "but I don't think she would see a need for it."

"You're not sure about it, so I'll leave it here until we can ask her. We'll take it out if she doesn't want it," said Christ. "Everyone who wants it has one."

"Can I see it?" asked Pastor Ansel.

"Absolutely," said the Lord. "Rose, would you show Pastor Almstedt Lydia's chapel, please?"

Quietly, Rose led Pastor Ansel into a small but comfortable room in the middle of a long corridor. She was glad for some time alone with her granddaughter's former pastor. She herself was very close to Jesus (at least He said so). She wondered whether Pastor Ansel could shed some light on where Lilly was spiritually.

"She's doing well in my opinion" was his response to Rose's inquiry. "I suggest you ask Christ though. He'd be able to tell you more than I would, Rose."

"I sure would." Jesus winked, suddenly appearing in the doorway of the chapel.

Rose ran to embrace Jesus.

"Enjoy each other's company for now." Jesus grinned, still holding her by the hand and gesturing toward Pastor Ansel. "We'll talk about Lily later."

"Do you like the chapel?" asked Rose, still breathless from being in the presence of the Lord.

"I do," remarked Pastor Ansel, surveying the room.

The chapel was pale green. There was an enormous grapevine cross against the back wall. It had a bouquet of yellow roses in the center of the cross. The bouquet was tied with a huge silk bow of the same color as the roses. There was a very ornate dark-stained altar made of oak. Both ends of the cloth-draped structure had a thick, wide-bottomed, white candle with tiny shavings of real gold melted into the wax.

There was no need for a lamp, for the glory of the Lord shone brightly in heaven (especially through the beautiful stained glass window). It depicted Jesus in the boat with His apostles during the storm. There was a tan recliner facing the altar several feet back. Two tapered candles stood on either side of the chair, each candle in a crystal holder atop an iron pole.

"Rose, you sit in the recliner. I'll get another one from the living room on this floor. If I'm going to be part of your family, I'd like to know you better," insisted Pastor Ansel.

He turned around in time to see Herman placing another recliner next to Rose.

"Thank you Herman, but I'm not helpless," commented Pastor Ansel.

"I was born Rose Ernestine Crenshaw to Joseph and Louise Crenshaw," she began. "I'm from Duluth originally. I went to school up there. My friends Audrey and Corryne would go skating with me when we were kids."

"When is your birthday?" asked Pastor Ansel.

"April 2." Rose chuckled. "My dad had my arrival planned for April 1, but I fooled him…After high school, I worked at B. W. Harris, making fur coats."

"When is your birthday?" inquired Rose.

"Actually, since heaven uses a Jewish lunar calendar, both of our birthdays are in the month of Adar II."

"You're smart. I bet you could be on a game show," concluded Rose enthusiastically. "It's surprising how much like earth heaven is."

"Yeah, except when people come through walls, and angels pull back the roof of your mansion and break into the 'Hallelujah' Chorus."

"We put some of Lloyd's artwork on the upper floors," Mary informed them. "She can have someone move them if there's a better place for them or if she doesn't want them."

"Oh, I'm sure Lydia will appreciate the thought, if nothing else," thought Pastor Ansel out loud. "I think the only way we would need to move them out is if we didn't have room for Alex's drawings."

"Have no concern about that," interjected Christ. "We deliberately left the walls on the lower floors—both here and in your own mansion—empty of any decoration so there would be space for your son's work. I can add rooms supernaturally whenever lack of space becomes an issue for any reason."

"Satisfy my curiosity about something."

"They're dancing out there again," Lloyd informed the small crowd that had gathered in the chapel.

They all heard the familiar tune of the Shaddish, a Swedish folk dance.

"Lord, do You help build the housing in heaven, or do You speak it into being?"

"Initially, I help design and build each one, but the additions are created through my speaking them into existence. We get a lot of help from the Amish people when it comes to the construction of the mansions around here. Trouble is… they're accustomed to modest, useful buildings. I hear one of them say, '*Hochmut*' when they start the architecture of a mansion…Here's a quilt that some of the Amish women made for Lydia."

"Amish people are saved?"

"Some of them are, and some aren't, Rose," answered Lloyd, entering midconversation.

"Wait, those are wedding rings on the quilt," observed Pastor Ansel, staring at it momentarily. "The Bible says there's no marriage in heaven."

"There's marriage another way," answered Christ.

"You and the church, right?"

"Correct."

"You and Lydia, like every other married couple whose marriage ended by the death of a spouse, will have a unique relationship with Me."

"What if they were married more than once?" Pastor Ansel smiled.

"Wait and see. Some answers must wait till the consummation of time on the old earth." Jesus smiled with a glint in His eye.

Pastor Ansel returned the smile, laughing a little at the mysterious side of the Lord.

Pastor Ansel's Colleagues

Pastor Ansel carefully looked over the written testimonies of his colleagues for signs of backsliding or things they believed on earth that were not biblical. For Pastor Stephen Kent, he gave a list of Bible verses on hell after a brief discussion of the fact that it wasn't originally intended for humans but for the devil and his angels. Now though it was reserved for not only the worst of humanity but for anyone who neglected to see Christ as a substitute for their own eternal death.

Jesus was the *only* way to remove the curse of Adam and Eve's first sin, even for good people. His colleague had explained that he was afraid of emptying the church with a "hell, fire, and brimstone" sermon once a month.

"Better to have an altar call"—Pastor Ansel shrugged—"than to send wonderful people to hell just because they didn't know Jesus."

Christ suddenly appeared, standing at the corner of Pastor Ansel's desk in Yeshua University.

"You will lose members," the Lord sternly told the other pastor. "Count on it! But others—some unsaved—will come. Better to speak the Truth—even only once to every person who walks through the doors of your building—than to be held accountable in part for their awful destiny.

"I don't want people to sit for an hour of empty ritual if all they are to do for Me is warm the pew with their behinds. They might let people who want to worship deeply and work for me have their spot."

Pastor Ansel noted that the word *church* was missing from Jesus's discussion of Pastor Kent's place of work.

"When He showed me my review," said Sam Gibbon's, one of Pastor Ansel's student pastors, "Jesus spoke so harshly. He told me not to make my pulpit a playpen."

"That was very stern," admitted Pastor Ansel. "You should have done more than assist the Holy Spirit in leading people to Christ. You should disciple them too."

"According to the information I received from the Lord concerning you," He states, "Neither My Father nor I were ever given credit for much in this man's life. I've given him salvation. Due to the unrepentant sin of pride prior to his review, I can offer him little in the way of reward."

"Psychology class taught me that you have to know yourself before you know Christ so you don't become schizophrenic. My psychology class also taught that denying yourself was an outdated idea."

"No, that's not right." Pastor Ansel sighed. "What made you choose a secular college for your undergraduate work?"

"It was what I could afford," explained Pastor Ansel's student.

"You give the name of the seminary you attended in your written testimony."

"Christ tells me it wasn't a good one."

"They were more interested in how you performed in front of a congregation than what the will of our Lord was," sighed Pastor Ansel.

After a pause that seemed to his charge like an eternity, Pastor Ansel began, "Tell you what…You seem like the kind of person who wholeheartedly wants to please God. You were just greatly misinformed. I know a couple people here who gladly intercede for you with respect to your pastoral position here."

"Who would they be?" asked Pastor Gibbons with the quick curiosity of a cat.

"You know that Jesus is always making intercession for the Church Militant?"

"Yes. I admit I'd forgotten. Jesus is the only one I need."

"I'm pleased to hear that you see Me as all sufficient," said Jesus with a smile.

"It is as You say."

"Yet I give one more person willing to stand in your defense."

"Who?"

"Your teacher, Pastor Ansel Almstedt."

"Lord, in my opinion, this man developed wrong assumptions about himself and You because of a terrible use of psychology. I think with a dip in the River and further training here at the university, at least some of his works can be restored."

"One thing I must add," insisted Christ. "You're going back to earth in an hour—earth time. During the rest of your time on earth, if you choose to study and take to heart everything in the Bible, if you tell others about Me, and, when you sin, come to Me and repent with sincerity, there will be some works that will not be burned when you come back to stay."

"I want to stay!" the man pleaded desperately. "They also taught me in psych class that there are people that are so heavenly minded that they're no earthly good."

"That's not biblical," replied Pastor Ansel. "It's one of Satan's lies."

"He speaks the truth," Jesus said of Pastor Ansel as the three of them sat by the bank of the River of Life. "I have a couple Scripture references I'd like you to memorize. Then we'll go for a swim.

"'If ye then be risen with Christ, seek those things which are above, where Christ sitteth on the right hand of God. Set your affection on things above, not on things on the earth.'"

"Let's turn back to John 14:6 [KJV]. Read it with me," instructed Pastor Ansel. "'Jesus saith unto him, I am the Way, the Truth, and the Life: no man cometh unto the Father, but by Me.'"

"Why are we gonna swim?"

"Bad memories of earth fade away when you swim in the River of Life. Besides, it's fun! I enjoyed it immensely," coaxed Pastor Ansel. "Jesus is coming too."

Relieved at thought of the Lord coming, Pastor Ansel's new friend took a fearless leap into the water.

After their swim, Jesus departed from them for a while.

Back in his mansion, Pastor Ansel made his way to the chapel. Once there, he breathed a prayer of thanks to God for the colleagues Christ had entrusted to his care, especially the last of them.

Pastor Ansel implored the Holy Spirit to correct this man's thinking so he wouldn't misinform his congregation about the existence of hell when the pastor went back to earth. He had very carefully taken each of them through the book of John, putting extra emphasis on the third chapter.

"Ansel, you've done everything you can. It's in My hands now," said Jesus, standing at his side.

"I've even tried flash cards with a Bible verse on each one about hell…What's our next move, Lord?" asked Pastor Ansel with a smile.

"Believe it or not, he's starting to take to heart everything you've said."

"Great! Then there's no more to do for him," assessed Pastor Ansel cheerfully.

"One more thing is necessary if your work with him isn't going to come unraveled on earth."

"What is that?"

"Come back to the university with Me. He's waiting there for us."

Instantly Pastor Ansel found himself standing with Jesus at the college's observatory deck, which was part of the hall that connected his office with the others on that floor.

"Turn around. It isn't necessary for you to see what's about to happen."

Immediately Pastor Ansel felt the presence of the Holy Spirit stronger than at any time since he'd come to heaven. His presence was confirmed by the appearance of a dove and a blinding light emanating from the Lord. Next to him, however, was one of his colleagues, experiencing a vision of hell.

"Look hard!" commanded Jesus, holding Pastor Kent by the shoulders like a vise.

It was deathly hot, with absolutely no water. What few trees he saw there were dead. He saw no grass there. The atmosphere reeked of sulfur. Deep foreboding darkness could be seen and felt. Countless numbers of people in the biggest fire pit shrieked in pain. Certain people there were in their own fire pit.

Fire in hell was dim. Fire burned people down to the bone, but they weren't consumed. Those who mocked the cross of

Jesus were hung on burning crosses. Some spared from the fire were eaten by worms. Everyone there longed for physical death, but it never came.

"What's that!" shrieked Pastor Kent in terror.

"It's a rat," said Christ, seemingly unmoved by the sight of the huge rodent.

"It looks like a small dog!"

"Not something you want to mess with," Jesus answered matter-of-factly. "Their bite is nasty."

Two insane woman ran into Pastor Kent's view.

"What's wrong with them?"

He trembled violently, only able to utter a hiss. He vomited, as a visible demon came into view. His throw up was black.

"Their punishment for eternity is to be chased by demons," explained his Savior.

He let out a howl of anguish as he suddenly recognized that one of the women he'd just seen had been his mother on earth. Just as quickly as the vision had occurred, it ended.

"She was a good woman." Stephen weeped softly.

Pastor Ansel noticed that his colleague was calmer now. The dove came to rest on the shoulder of his pupil.

"Oh, I know," agreed Christ. "I'm deeply saddened that such a one never asked Me to become their Savior. Without regeneration, good works mean nothing. Now, I give one final warning. When you go back to earth, take careful note of the fact that about a third of your congregation is unsaved, partly due to your bad preaching."

The Lord held the man's face tenderly in His nail-scarred hands. "Tell them they're going to hell. I'll take your church away if you don't cooperate with Me.

"Ansel, take him to My mansion. Help him take a shower, and put him to bed. He's still recovering from his horrific ordeal. Give him a couple glasses of cold water to drink. The Holy Spirit will show you where to find My place as well as everything else you need."

"King David will stop by to play the harp for him. He loves music. It will soothe his nerves. When David is through, read him some gentle, reassuring passages from the Bible."

"Yes, Lord, right away. May I ask you something?"

Jesus nodded, regarding Pastor Ansel with warm affection.

"Wouldn't he rather see his own mansion?"

"Yes, but he isn't due here for a year, so his own mansion isn't finished yet," explained Yeshua.

"Why is he here now then?" asked Pastor Ansel.

"He had a heart attack," replied Jesus. "His diet was atrocious. When he wakes up from his nap, you can take him over there."

"Okay." Pastor Ansel laughed with sheer joy. "Come with me. Let's follow the dove."

13

The Master's Mansion

They arrived within seconds though the Master's mansion was a considerable distance from the city—nestled comfortably in an enormous green valley between two mountains. It was a chalet with a large bay window in the first floor living room.

"Where to now, Holy Spirit?" inquired Pastor Ansel silently after they'd entered through the front door.

They were led up to the third floor.

"Pastor Almstedt, when I had that vision of hell, the Lord hid from my mind the fact that I was saved."

"Yes…There must be a Bible around here somewhere," pondered Pastor Ansel out loud. "I prefer the New International Version. I think it's much easier to understand than the King James Version."

"My paternal grandmother always read to us from the King James," the other pastor said.

He quoted from Hebrews 12:6, "'For whom the Lord loveth he chasteneth, and scourgeth every son whom he receiveth.'"

Pastor Ansel said, "You see, the Holy Spirit showed you that verse to let you understand that with a different theology on hell, you can be a much wiser person. He loves you whether you do or not. You don't want to be dishonest especially about something as serious as hell.

"It's hard to tell someone that they're going to hell if they don't receive Christ as their personal Savior, but it's better than having them go there. If you preach the truth, there's always the possibility that someone will hear you and respond."

Pastor Ansel became silent momentarily so that his companion could absorb what he just said.

"I'll start running your water, unless you'd rather rest first?"

"What good did that truth do my mother?"

"When you changed your view on hell, is that when your mother died?" asked Pastor Ansel, giving his colleague a hug. "Whatever you or I believe about hell, it doesn't change the fact that it's there. You know that now."

"I witnessed to my mother every day since I was saved, but she didn't listen," sighed Pastor Ansel's new friend.

"Pray that you'll be able to let go," instructed Pastor Ansel. "It's not your responsibility to convert. That's up to the Holy Spirit."

Sleep came slowly for the cleric. Christ gradually took away the terror from his mind, but the memory was still there. He had insisted on wanting to shower by himself, but heeding the Holy Spirit's warning, Pastor Ansel didn't leave him alone.

———

Pastor Ansel was in the middle of reading a Scripture when his colleague woke up. He recognized the familiar verse. It was Psalm 30:5.

> For his anger lasts only a moment, but his favor lasts a lifetime; weeping may stay for the night, but rejoicing comes in the morning.

"Here's one that my friend Lilly likes."

> And you also were included in Christ when you heard the message of truth, the gospel of your salvation. When you believed, you were marked in him with a seal, the promised Holy Spirit, who is a deposit guaranteeing our inheritance until the redemption of those who are God's possession—to the praise of his glory. (Eph. 1:13–14)

Pastor Ansel continued.

> Your word is a lamp for my feet, / a light on my path. (Ps. 119:105)

Therefore, there is now no condemnation for those who are in Christ Jesus... (Rom. 8:1)

Who shall separate us from the love of Christ? Shall trouble or hardship or persecution or famine or nakedness or danger or sword? (Rom.8:35)

No, in all these things we are more than conquerors through him who loved us. For I am convinced that neither death nor life, neither angels nor demons, neither the present nor the future, nor any powers, neither height nor depth, nor anything else in all creation, will be able to separate us from the love of God that is in Christ Jesus our Lord. (Rom. 8:37–39)

"Hello, Mary." Pastor Ansel smiled as she came through the wall of Christ's bedroom. Pastor Ansel was relieved to see Jesus following, almost at her heels.

"You can go now if you like," said the Lord. "Mother and I are here."

"Yesh, I'll brew some tea for him."

"Sounds wonderful."

"Where can I find animal food?" asked Pastor Ansel, leaning on the doorway of the Lord's room.

"Selah and Gloria already got some for both Bear and Mia. Herman put it in the pantry of your kitchen," answered Jesus.

14

Game Time

"**N**ice. Where can I find a gun? I've got a taste for some venison."

"You've got a deer rifle above the fireplace on the gun rack in your cabin."

"I have a cabin too?" exclaimed Pastor Ansel joyfully.

"You do."

"Wow! You didn't have to give me as much as you have."

"I know. But in My humble opinion, you've earned everything you've gotten from Me. Remember, no shooting on the third level. And when you hunt, you can take Bear with you but not Mia. In the second heaven, gunfire would scare her."

"Where is the cabin?"

"Very near here. In the valley basin. I'll take you there if you like," offered Christ.

Guided by the Holy Spirit, Pastor Ansel walked toward the valley (though if they had wanted, they could have been there in a matter of seconds).

———

It was large, for a cabin. Each log was split in half, the flat side facing inward. Unlike his mansion, which had eight floors, this dwelling had only three floors and an attic. Still, each room here was larger than those in the mansion by a considerable degree.

Rectangular windows surrounded the only living room, which was the size of two rooms. There was a high ceiling, which had a fan spinning on it. Hung above the fireplace, as the Lord had promised, was a gun suitable for hunting and a moose head with glass eyes. Each end of the cabin's enormous entryway had four couches of varying earth tones and a recliner on both ends, as well.

"Did you have any more work for me to do today, or can I track a deer?"

"Go hunt and have fun."

"Three days from now, earth time, Frank Hale will be here."

"Praise God!" blurted Pastor Ansel suddenly as he recognized a well-known member of another congregation he'd pastored. "No more ALS for him."

"True," whispered the Holy Spirit. "Thank you for your praise."

"He's asked Me in prayer if he can have some time with you when he comes here," said Jesus.

"I'm guessing You told him that would be just fine."

"I did," answered Christ.

"Is it a social call?" asked Pastor Ansel. "I'll tell him about bringing down a ten-point buck."

"He wants to study the Bible with you, but he'll mention baseball too."

They both laughed hard, knowing how much Frank enjoyed the sport. Pastor Ansel remembered how the discussion of it often brought a smile to his face in spite of the severity of his illness.

"Give Me your thoughts on this, Ansel. What would you think if I made Frank a manager of one of our baseball teams here in the third heaven?"

"First, I'd like to thank You for confiding in me. Makes me feel like Moses, a real friend. Second, I didn't know there were baseball teams here. Scripture doesn't say anything about baseball."

"Why do people see heaven as either an eternal church service or folks sitting on a cloud, strumming a harp all day? There are many things to do here—too many to fit them all in the Bible. And you never answered My question."

"Lord, I don't know if he has the skill to manage a team, but I trust Your judgment. If You think he's capable of doing it, by all means, let him.

By the way, when are we going to give those gifts to the Chinese families here whose relatives are at Jesus, Friend of Sinners Baptist Church?"

"Here's a list of all the people we want to give presents to. Be sure to let them know the names of their earthly family members whose prayers resulted in them receiving the gift. It wasn't mentioned in conversation at lunch yesterday, but I also have gifts for the families of the Korean congregation here, as well."

Pastor Ansel looked with awe at the wide array of gifts in the particular storehouse they went to. They gathered armloads of precious items. Each present had a tag with a specific person's name on it. They ranged from (but were not limited to) ethnic clothing, tapestries, embroidered hankies, silk tablecloths, games, and other toys.

"Thank you for help," said Christ. "Would you like to help with the distribution of these things?"

"I sure would."

"Okay, I'll get the wrapping paper and meet you at My place."

Pastor Ansel and the Lord returned to the valley on the second level long before the sunset. The Master went to check on the rogue clergyman, and Pastor Ansel went to get his rifle.

Jesus found Pastor Kent sitting up in bed, surrounded by many children. They were absorbed in a card game, the cards for which Lloyd Peace had done the design (both front and back). His granddaughter Lilly held the copyright for the game.

"Each card has a Bible person on it," explained Brian. "There are four of the same person in all the cards, 'cept Jesus. There's one card with Him on it. You have to get four of all the other ones to win and have the card with Jesus on it."

"Why did you come here?" asked Pastor Kent of Brian.

"I died in my mommy's tummy," Brian answered somberly. "It's your turn."

The pastor laid down his last pile of four cards. (Each pile was known as a book.) He smiled, showing the little ones the coveted Jesus card.

—◦◦◦—

Pastor Ansel rejoiced to feel a deer stand under him again. He held the gun with the skill of someone who'd handled a weapon many times before. He looked through the scope at a huge buck.

"One bullet to the heart ought to drop him," muttered Pastor Ansel to himself.

He pulled the trigger, and watched the deer fall. He was relieved it was a clean shot.

"How's my colleague doing?" asked Pastor Ansel of Jesus, who was standing next to him.

"He's going to be all right. He was sent back to earth for further sanctification."

Jesus reached out and touched the animal; and the deer rose to its feet, giving Pastor Ansel a mean look and a snort.

"You healed my food," said Pastor Ansel, annoyed with the deer.

"Yes. You were allowed to have the fun of shooting it. Herman put half a dozen deer in the pantry of your mansion. Your cabin pantry is well stocked with venison too. You can shoot another one when your supply is low."

"Part of the fun of hunting—like fishing—is eating your trophy."

"True," replied the Lord. "And if you must, I will give that beast into your hands. Do with him as you wish."

"No," responded Pastor Ansel. "I won't shoot him again… Why did you let Herman shoot so many? Herman is a beautiful guardian angel, but I'm not sure I trust him with a gun."

"Michael taught him everything he knows about handling a sword or firearm," Christ informed Pastor Ansel.

"You taught Your archangel to shoot? I'm impressed. But how do you preserve raw meat in a pantry?"

"Cold food stays cold, and hot food stays hot in the third heaven. Most people in the third heaven have modern appliances, even though they don't need them. It's just a matter of personal preference."

"What am I gonna do with all that meat?"

"It won't go to waste. Everything lasts in the third heaven." Jesus smiled broadly and nodded, taking His cell phone out of the pocket of His tunic.

"Lloyd, this is God. You can meet Pastor Ansel and me at the restaurant."

Pastor Ansel chucked at the Lord being so formal with Himself for the sake of humor.

"Ask the apostle Paul to come as well."

15

The Restaurant

Seconds later, back in the third heaven, they were sitting in one of two eating establishments in that realm. They ordered burgers just as Lloyd, Rose, and Brian walked in.

"Lloyd," Jesus began, "sorry to take away business from your boarding house."

"One meal at this restaurant isn't going to ruin us financially during the Millennium," answered Lloyd.

"Pastor Ansel likes to hunt, fish, and camp out. Would he and I be a good candidate for your hiking club Rose?" Jesus grinned.

"Yes!" she said wholeheartedly.

"Provided we can stay in the third heaven when we hike, I'd love to hike with your club," agreed Pastor Ansel. "What are the requirements for membership?"

"There were mandatory dues for each member on earth, but now it's a free-will offering," answered Lloyd. "There's no money here, but during the Millennium, we will be paid."

"What will you do with the money, Grandma?"

"We would save it for a year and vote on how to spend it at the end of the year," explained Rose.

"What does 'vote' mean, Paul?" Brian asked inquisitively.

"I'll show you what I mean. Watch what happens when I say this…Who thinks Brian should have milk? Raise your hand."

Paul and Lloyd raised their hands.

"Who thinks Brian should have pop?" asked the apostle.

Jesus, Rose, and Brian raised their hands.

"You can't vote, Brian." The server laughed, taking the menus. "They're voting about you."

"Paul, why did you vote for milk?" a disappointed Brian said.

"Your body is a place where the Holy Spirit lives. You should take care of it."

"Rose, you're gonna spoil him," scolded Lloyd, "the way you did Lilly."

"You spoiled her a little too, Lloyd." Rose frowned.

"All right, we both spoiled Lilly. I spoiled her sisters too. We're Brian's grandparents, but until Will and Joy come, we're his guardians too. We can't ruin him. Will and Joy will have a fit," Lloyd admonished Rose gently.

"Neither of you have nor will ruin him," interjected Christ. "There's no sin in the third heaven. Let him have the soda."

"Jesus what does *ruin* mean?" asked Brian.

"Children on earth who get whatever they want all the time are ruined as grown-ups because there's sin on earth, Brian."

"See, Rose," insisted Christ, "Brian isn't so high-spirited to drive anyone crazy. He's just full of the Holy Spirit. He's full of joy because of it."

"Do you want Coke or Pepsi? Let me tell you something, Brian." The server winked in the direction of the boy. "Jesus is the boss here in the universe. If He says you can have something, it doesn't matter how anyone else votes."

"One of each please," the youngster replied.

The server looked at the Lord for his approval.

"That would be fine. Coke in honor of his friend Pastor Ansel and his sister Natalie. Pepsi in honor of his sisters Carley and Lilly."

"Yes!" squealed Brian, clapping for joy and rubbing his grandmother's upper arm repeatedly with affection.

16

The Peace's at Home

It was agreed by all that they would all hike to the throne room outside the city, near the mountain furthest away from Pastor Ansel's cabin. Paul told Pastor Ansel at length about what it was like to be a missionary, how loved he was by the Ephesian converts, and how the church at Philippi was so generous with their money and other gifts when he was in prison there for worshiping Christ. Rose and Lloyd also shared more about themselves.

"What else—in addition to dancing—can I do for heaven's festival?" asked Pastor Ansel.

"You can carry the American flag with Brian," replied Jesus. "There is also ethnic craft booths and ethnic food stands."

"Can I do all four?" Pastor Ansel asked delightedly.

"You sure can," answered Rose, Lloyd, and Christ, one after the other while they put up many enormous tents that Paul had made for heaven's hiking club.

The one thousand people in the hike stayed in the valley for a while. They all prayed collectively and privately. Jesus gratefully received their worship. Frank Hale and Pastor Ansel, who had enjoyed each other's company earlier that day, now stood together in silence. They watched an eagle fly overhead.

Pastor Ansel finally broke the stillness.

"Frank, Pastor Brent would love to here those jazz CDs that the Lord gave you."

"I'll see to it that he gets that opportunity."

The two men looked at each other, remembering how Christ was transfigured before them in Frank's mansion that day. Without warning, the music stopped, the roof disappeared (temporarily), and the Father said, "This is My beloved Son, with whom I'm well pleased."

"I love you both."

"My brother Will would like to listen to jazz CDs, Master," said Lulu.

"I know. That's why I put some in his mansion." The Lord hugged her.

"Michael, what is it?" probed the Savior.

"Did you hear Brian Peace's prayer to have a private audience with You, Pastor Ansel, and all heaven's children? Seraph is with them now," Michael informed Jesus.

Pastor Ansel recognized Seraph as Brian's guardian angel. One of things that brought Brian joy was the fact that Seraph was one of the angels that appeared to the shepherds at Christmas.

"Seraph was actually Seraphim. She was too humble to even want a name," explained the boy to the others as Yeshua and Pastor Ansel walked into the throne room, opposite the mountain on the far side of the valley.

"We're here, children," spoke Jesus gently.

He and Pastor Ansel held the face of each child tenderly in their hands and greeted each one in his or her own language.

"Brian, since you called this prayer vigil, why don't you start?" suggested Pastor Ansel.

"Thank You for dying and coming to life again. "Please help Lilly to tell people, especially my sister Natalie, that they need You to be their Savior so they can know You and come to heaven. Please help Natalie to be straightened out so she can come to heaven."

He was tapped on the shoulder by a little girl named Rosemary.

"You mean she needs to be straight," whispered the pretty red-haired girl.

She had an egg-shaped face with freckles. Her brown eyes met those of Jesus. He held an index finger up to His mouth, stifling her giggle. Christ smiled at her.

"Please let my sister Carley listen to only wise things that people say," Brian pleaded earnestly on behalf of his sisters.

Jesus walked over to Brian. "What about your parents?"

He prayed for them silently. Each child, in turn, prayed however the Spirit led them.

"My sisters are beautiful, Makiko," Pastor Ansel heard Brian say as the crowd of children left the throne room.

Pastor Ansel was touched that all the kids remembered to include his earthly family in their petitions.

"We know that your sisters are beautiful." Makiko and her twin sister, Mako, laughed tenderly.

—◆◆◆—

Back in the valley, Pastor Ansel and Christ rejoined the hikers. Come the next day, the Master, Pastor Ansel, and others would first head in the direction they had come. Together they would conquer the mountain on foot. Rather than scale down on the throne room side (since the two of them had already been there), it was decided by the whole club that they would meet at Rose Peace's mansion and eat some of the venison that Herman had prepared.

Both Lloyd and Rose set aside an office for Pastor Ansel in their mansion. During the prime-time game shows on TV, Pastor Ansel excused himself. He sat at the small desk and wrote a note to Friend of Sinners Baptist Church.

> Pastor Ansel Almstedt, servant of God, and the Lord Jesus Christ
>
> I thank my God upon all my remembrance of you.

Stand firm in Christ and don't be afraid. Jesus is with you. Though I am no longer physically present with you, I watch over you as does Christ. I've been told the welcome never stops here in the third heaven. I testify to the truth of this.

With all of you, I eagerly await the consummation of the church when I will join those of you who have asked Jesus to be your Savior.

Praise be to the Lord Jesus Christ forever and ever and ever! Amen.